Grandpa's Third Drawer

University of Nebraska Press

LINCOLN

Grandpa's Third Drawer

UNLOCKING HOLOCAUST MEMORIES

Written and illustrated by Judy Tal Kopelman

The Jewish Publication Society

PHILADELPHIA

Hebrew-language edition, *Hamegera Hashleesheet
Shel Saba*, © 2003 by Miscal-Yediot Achronot Books
and Chemed Books
All rights reserved. Published by the University of
Nebraska Press as a Jewish Publication Society book.
Manufactured in China.

The objects and documents shown in the illustrations
are courtesy of Beit Theresienstadt Archives, Givat-Haim
Ichud, Israel.

Library of Congress Cataloging-in-Publication Data

Tal, Judy.
[Megerah ha-shelishit shel saba. English]
Grandpa's third drawer: unlocking Holocaust memories /
written and illustrated by Judy Tal Kopelman.
pages   cm
Summary: "Young Uri finds the key to his grandpa's
locked drawer and discovers poignant mementos from
the Holocaust"—Provided by publisher.
ISBN 978-0-8276-1204-4 (cloth: alk. paper)
ISBN 978-0-8276-1221-1 (pbk.: alk. paper)
ISBN 978-0-8276-1170-2 (epub)
ISBN 978-0-8276-1171-9 (mobi)
ISBN 978-0-8276-1169-6 (pdf)
1. Holocaust, Jewish (1939–1945)—Juvenile fiction. I. Title.
PZ7.TI4139GR 2014   [E]—dc23   2013031274

Designed and set in Scala by A. Shahan.

To Arik

Thanks to Yoel
for the drawing
on page vi

Of all the places in the world, I love to stay at Grandma Genia and Grandpa Yuda's house. I spend all my vacations there—away from my nagging sister, away from my parents—without ever having to wake up early, without having to go to school.

Grandpa Yuda—he's my best friend. He always has time to play with me.

Grandma Genia—she makes me yummy hot chocolate and bakes my favorite cookies. Sometimes she sits with us and knits quietly.

There's a kind of quiet in Grandma and Grandpa's house. It's the silence of people who come from a faraway world—a vanished world that still lives in memories.

Of all the rooms in my grandparents' house, I prefer to play in Grandpa's study, where he keeps his desk, his piano, and lots of other stuff.

Grandpa's desk has three drawers.

In the first drawer, Grandpa keeps his pens and paper. My pencil case and favorite crayons are also there.

The second drawer has all sorts of special old toys that are made of wood or metal. Grandpa used to play with them when he was a boy before the war. When Grandpa had to leave his house in Germany, his neighbors kept his toy box for him until the war was over.

The third drawer of his desk is always locked. No one ever opens it . . .

I wonder why it is forbidden . . .

*B*reakfast at Grandpa and Grandma's lasts for as long as you like. The wonderful smell of freshly baked bread fills the house. Grandma sets the table with beautifully decorated china and crocheted napkins. There are all sorts of special ornaments in the house: Grandma's handmade tablecloths, pretty glass vases, and paintings of spectacular landscapes.

The morning sun shines through the curtains, creating spots of light on the tablecloth. Sometimes a ray of light slips in, and you can see thousands of dust particles floating in midair.

*A*fter breakfast, we usually spend time in Grandpa's study.

I like to take my crayons from the first drawer of his desk and draw. I can draw for as long as I want, and no one tries to snatch the crayons away from me. I also love playing with Grandpa's old toys—the ones in the second drawer.

But I always look at the third drawer and wonder what's inside it. Why am I not allowed to open it?

When we are together, Grandpa likes to listen to music. He doesn't listen to the news or read the paper. He has an old record player on which he plays his favorite music by Mozart and Beethoven.

Sometimes he'll sit and play the piano.

Grandpa says that playing Mozart makes him feel like he lives in a perfect world. When he plays, his eyes sparkle. He looks into the distance as if he were somewhere else.

Perhaps he thinks about days long gone, when he was a boy like me.

BEETHOVEN

Symphonien zu 4 I

Symphonies à 4 mains — Symphonie

Band I. No. 1–5.

(Ulrich.)

LA VOCE DEL PADR

On Grandpa's table in the corner, there's a special box for chocolates that Grandma and Grandpa brought from Germany. When I feel like having a sweet, I take a peek to find out what's inside. Sometimes I find caramel candies and sometimes Belgian chocolate. Yum!

Grandma says that chocolate needs to be freshly made out of pure ingredients, using a recipe passed on from generation to generation. Grandma loves to spoil me. When I take a sweet, she always says, "Have another!"

When I play with Grandpa's toys from the second drawer in the desk, I try to imagine him as a boy. There are a few photos in the drawer—of Grandpa when he was a child, of the magnificent house he grew up in, and of family trips to the countryside.

There is also one of his sister, Anna, whom I never knew.

Once, I asked Grandpa to take me to Germany. He didn't want to, I think.

"Perhaps one day," he said.

*D*uring my last visit to my grandparents' house in the winter, there was one cold and rainy day when Grandma and Grandpa went out for a bit, and I stayed at the house on my own.

In Grandpa's study, I opened the first desk drawer to get my crayons and pencil case, and I suddenly noticed a key hiding in the corner of the drawer!

I was sure that this key opened the third drawer, the one that's always locked. The forbidden one.

I couldn't help myself.

I turned the key in the keyhole and barely managed to open it.

It smelled awful . . . like the locked-away place that it was.

At that very moment I heard Grandma and Grandpa come into the house. Grandpa entered the study and saw me sitting by the open drawer.

"What are you doing?!" he said, raising his voice. It startled me. Grandpa is always so calm. I was holding a yellow Star of David attached to a rusty pin.

"I can't get this thing to open!" I said and began to cry.

"This isn't a game!" he yelled and grabbed the yellow star from my hand.

"I want to go home!" I cried. "I want Mommy and Daddy to come and get me!"

Grandpa sat down on his chair and closed his eyes. He drew me close and held me.

"Uri, I'm sorry. You shouldn't see this . . ." he said quietly.

"What, Grandpa? What is all this stuff? These strange things—are they yours?" I asked.

"Not only mine," he replied. "All right. Here, come, I'll tell you."

"When I was a boy in Germany, there were hard times. The Nazis came to power. They sent us all to live in the ghetto, behind a high wall in old, crowded houses. We were forced to wear this yellow Star of David. It marked us Jews as . . . inferior outcasts who were forbidden to leave the ghetto."

"Grandpa, I don't understand," I said. "They drove you away from your home and all of your toys?"

"Yes, Uri," Grandpa said. "We were forced from our homes and had to leave everything behind us."

Grandpa began taking things out of the drawer.

"This doll belonged to my beautiful sister, Anna. In the ghetto, we had no toys, so my mother sewed this doll for her from rags. Anna really loved it. She carried it with her all the time."

I touched the doll.

"These are stamps from the ghetto. For them, we were given very small portions of food, usually bread and potatoes. We were hungry, very hungry, all the time. There were many children there about my age, sick and weak from hunger."

Grandpa took out a wooden box from the drawer. It had dominoes in it.

"These I made with my own two hands from a piece of wood I found in the street. We would play with them for hours, Anna and I. That is how we kept a seed of happiness in our hearts," said Grandpa in his funny German accent. He smiled a bit.

Grandma was standing by the door, and she was smiling too.

"Then one day, the Nazi soldiers divided all the Jews of the ghetto into groups and sent us by train to many different places. My grandfather and grandmother were sent to a concentration camp along with all the older people. My sister and my parents were sent somewhere else on another train. I was sent to work in a labor camp with many other young men."

Grandpa took a small notebook from the drawer.

"This is the diary Anna kept when we were in the ghetto. She wrote these last few pages before they put her on the train. I took it with me in order to give it back to her when we were together again . . ."

"And did you?" I asked.

"No," Grandpa said sadly. "I've never seen her since. Nor my parents or my grandparents . . . I never saw them again. I was alone in the camp. I was tired and hungry and sad . . ."

This was the first time I had ever seen Grandpa cry.

We went to sleep very late that night.

I asked Grandpa so many questions. About Anna, about the ghetto, about the camp, about the Nazis, about Germany . . .

We set up Grandpa's domino game on the dining room table. We played one game, then another, then another, just as Anna and Grandpa used to play in the ghetto.

When we got tired, we placed all the domino pieces so they were standing side by side next to each other.

I flicked the first one and all the rest fell one by one, TICK, TICK, TICK . . .

Then we took out the remaining things from the drawer and looked at all of them.

I never knew that Grandpa was such a brave kid.

I never knew what he'd been through.

Now, I love him even more.